This book
belongs to

....

Five-minute Forest Tales

Written by
Catherine Veitch

MILES KELLY

For Sonya. I hope your pupils enjoy listening to these stories – thanks for the suggestion – C.V

First published in 2020 by Miles Kelly Publishing Ltd
Harding's Barn, Bardfield End Green, Thaxted, Essex, CM6 3PX, UK

2 4 6 8 10 9 7 5 3 1

Publishing Director Belinda Gallagher
Creative Director Jo Cowan
Editorial Director Rosie Neave
Design Managers Joe Jones, Simon Lee
Image Manager Liberty Newton
Production Elizabeth Collins, Jennifer Brunwin-Jones
Reprographics Stephan Davis
Assets Lorraine King
Cover Artist Elissambura at Advocate Art

ISBN 978-1-78989-072-3

Printed in China

British Library Cataloguing-in-Publication Data
A catalogue record for this book is available from the British Library

Made with paper from a sustainable forest

www.mileskelly.net

Contents

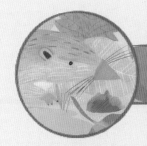

CoLOURfUL
FoRests

Forests can change colour throughout the year. In autumn, leaves are red, gold and orange. Spring brings blossom and bright, buzzing insects. Summer forests may be heavy with fruit and flowers. All kinds of animals live in these forests of colour. Shall we meet some of them?

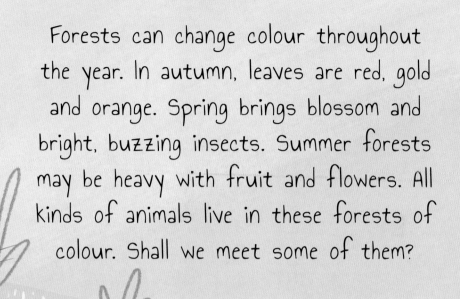

The Detective Deer

Illustrated by Lucy Barnard

It was springtime, and many animals and plants were waking up after their long winter sleep. The forest was bursting with flowers and new shoots, and animals were busy building homes.

Diamond and Denzel were twin white-tailed deer. They were playing with an old bird's nest whilst their

Kick!

mother went off to graze.
The nest shot into a
tree hole. "Grrrrrrr!"

"What's that? No one lives there, Walter the woodpecker moved out last week," said Diamond. This was a mystery, and Diamond loved solving mysteries.

"Grrrrrrr!" went the hole again.

Let's get some help!

The twins found Cruz, a hungry chipmunk, stuffing his face with nuts he had stored over winter.

"I cank awlk ow," said Cruz with his mouth full. But he followed the twins, grabbing some nuts to take with him.

Grrrr!

16

"Can you spit a nut into that hole?" asked Diamond. They waited as Cruz took aim... then **pop pop pop!** Cruz spat three nuts neatly into the hole!

"**Grrrr!**" went the hole.

"I told you to spit just one nut!" said Diamond.

"**Uh oh!**" replied Cruz, who was talking normally now.

I hope I get them back.

"Why won't it come out?" asked Denzel.
"I'll fetch Shelby," replied Diamond.
"Maybe he can help us to
solve this puzzle."

It did not take Diamond long to find
Shelby, her friend the grey squirrel. She
filled him in on the strange sounds that
had come from the hole as they made
their way back.

"Let me drop something in the
hole," Shelby suggested.

"Ready, aim, fire!"
shouted Diamond.

Shelby threw a catkin into the hole. They waited... but nothing happened. Shelby was just about to throw in another catkin, when a strange whistle came out of the hole. It was hard to hear at first, but then it got louder, and louder... until it was so loud that the animals ran away.

WheeZZZZZZZZZZ!

They ran so fast that they didn't spot a turtle who had just woken up from her winter sleep. She was warming herself in the sun.

Hey, watch where you're going!

Diamond told
the turtle, whose
name was Tiffany,
about the monster
in the hole.

"Why are big animals like you scared of
a whistling hole?" asked Tiffany. "I need to
see this hole. Can you take me?"

Tiffany was not the fastest walker and it took ages to walk back to the hole.

"Throw something in," said Diamond.

But Tiffany couldn't throw anything in.

"I can't reach the hole from here and I can't climb the tree," she said.

But as Diamond looked down at Tiffany, she spotted a clue.

"Look!" Diamond
pointed at Tiffany.
   "We can't throw Tiffany
in the hole!" said Denzel.
   But Diamond was
pointing to the tracks
on the muddy forest
floor around
Tiffany.

"If we match our feet to our tracks, the tracks left over will belong to the mystery monster in the hole!" It was a genius idea and the animals had fun finding their tracks.

So we know its tracks look like this.

The animals had worked out which tracks belonged to the mystery tree monster. But it did not help them guess its name.

"We all have different poos. Why don't we look for our poo and the odd poo out will belong to the tree monster!" said Denzel.

No one had a better idea, so the animals all looked for their poo. It was a smelly job!

EWW!

The animals worked out which poo belonged to the tree monster, but that did not help them guess its name either. They were about to give up when mother deer returned with some tasty shoots for her fawns.

Whilst tucking into them, the twins told their mother about their adventurous morning. She listened carefully and gave them an idea...

That night, the animals stayed up to watch the hole.

After dark, something moved inside. A catkin flew out, followed by some nuts and lastly a bird's nest. Then a face appeared. It looked like it was wearing mask. It was not a monster at all, but a sleepy raccoon who had moved in!

The mystery was solved. All of the animals welcomed their new neighbour. Although Tiffany stayed hidden, because raccoons sometimes eat turtles!

33

The FORGetful Elephant

Illustrated by
Giovana Medeiros

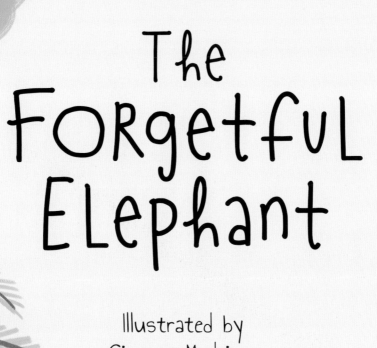

A young elephant called Ellery lived with his herd in the African rainforest. The leader of the herd was wise Earleen - she knew everything about the forest. She taught Ellery all about plants that could make him better when he was ill, and she often asked him to fetch them from the forest. But Ellery was quite a forgetful elephant.

One day,
Earleen took Ellery
to one side.
"Your sister has a
fever, and I need you to fetch
some bark from a tree that
has green seed pods."

38

So Ellery set off through the forest, but he hadn't gone far when he realized he had forgotten which tree to look for. All he could remember was that something beginning with the letters g and p was in the tree.

Squawk!

"It must be the tree over there with the grey parrot!" said Ellery. But the bark was hard to pull off.

"Can I help you?" asked an okapi called Olalla. Ellery explained his problem and Olalla easily pulled off some bark with her long tongue.

Ellery thanked Olalla and took the bark to Earleen. But oh dear, the bark was from the wrong tree!

Ellery! How can you be so forgetful?

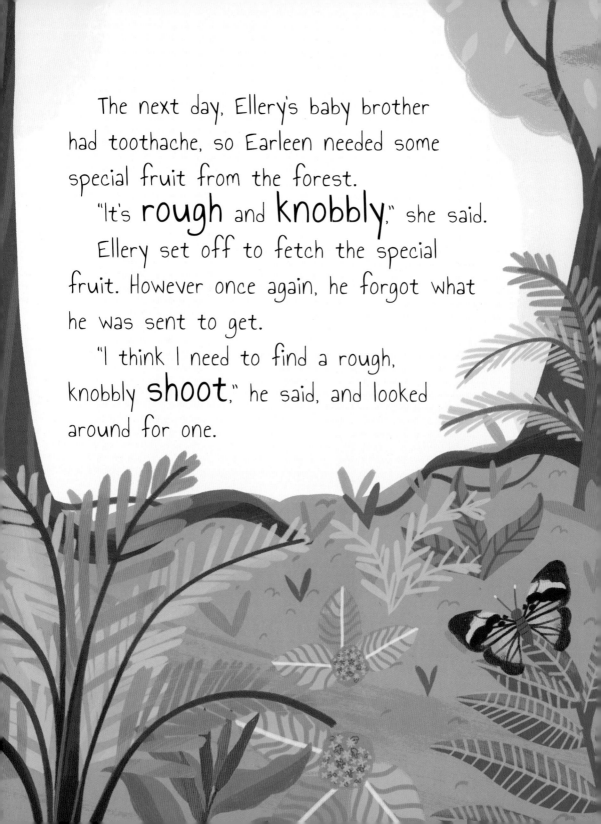

The next day, Ellery's baby brother had toothache, so Earleen needed some special fruit from the forest.

"It's **rough** and **knobbly**," she said.

Ellery set off to fetch the special fruit. However once again, he forgot what he was sent to get.

"I think I need to find a rough, knobbly **shoot**," he said, and looked around for one.

"This must be it," said Ellery. But the shoot was hard to tug out of the soil. He didn't notice he had an audience of bonobos! Ellery pulled and pulled... until at last...

SPLAT

Ha ha!

...the shoot was out! **Splat!** Ellery landed in a muddy pool.

What's so funny?

Ellery glared at the bonobos, and set off back to his herd.

"I asked you to get **fruit** not a **shoot**," said Earleen. "How are you going to survive in the forest when you grow up and leave the herd?" she asked.

Whoops...

A few days later, Earleen had a tummyache so she sent Ellery on another errand.

"Bring back some **juicy leaves** from one of the tallest trees in the forest," she said.

Stretch!

This time, Ellery remembered what Earleen had asked for. He soon found the tall tree with big, juicy leaves. But oh no! Such bad luck! He could not quite reach the leaves.

I just can't... quite... reach!

48

So Ellery tried to shake some
leaves off.
  He rammed the tree... smack!
  He tossed branches at it...
thwack!

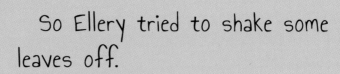

Swoosh!

And he sprayed water
at it... swoosh! But the
stubborn tree would not let
go of any leaves.

"Who's shaking my tree?" asked an angry colobus monkey called Cam. "I'm so sorry," said Ellery. Earleen had always taught him to be polite to strangers. He explained that he just wanted a few leaves.

Here, take these.

Eeek!

But all the shaking of the tree had woken a leopard, and it was creeping towards Cam. Ellery remembered that Earleen had told him to keep away from leopards.

Leopard! RUN!

Ellery had warned Cam just in time. She leapt onto the next tree, and the next, and the next after that, dropping Ellery's leaves as she went. The leopard could not catch her. Ellery was fast, too, but the leopard was chasing him.

"I must warn the herd," he gasped. He remembered that he could send them a message by drumming his feet on the ground. Th... thump, th...thump, th...thump, th...thump went Ellery's feet.

Thump! Thump!

In the distance, the herd felt the ground shake and picked up the message. As Ellery safely reached her, Earleen flapped her ears and raised her trunk.

Quick, Ellery, get behind me!

"Raaarrrr!" Earleen's roar was loud enough to wake every animal in the forest. The leopard knew he was no match for such a big elephant and slunk off.

"I remembered the juicy leaves from the tall tree but I couldn't reach them, and then the leopard showed up," Ellery sobbed.

Earleen did not mind because she was proud of Ellery for remembering that leopards were dangerous, and how to warn the herd by drumming his feet.

"You are not a forgetful elephant any more," said Earleen. "Well done for warning us of the danger. Let's celebrate by having a mud bath!"

Splat!

The Magnificent Butterfly

Illustrated by Julia Seal

One day, a caterpillar hatched from
a tiny egg. He ate lots of leaves and grew
and grew. When winter came, he hid himself
away and went to sleep.

Munch!

The warm spring woke him and he ate
more leaves.

Munch!

Munch!

When summer arrived
the caterpillar knew it
was time to change.
So he turned himself
into a chrysalis,
which looked just like
the leaf he hung
beneath. Inside, the
caterpillar began
to change into...

...A beautiful butterfly!

One day, when he was ready, the new butterfly emerged from the chrysalis and unfolded his wings. He was a purple emperor butterfly and his name was Blaze.

Throughout the forest there were whispers about a splendid new butterfly, and all the animals looked out for him. But Blaze was proud, and did not want to mix with the other animals.

Blaze was the talk
of the forest.
"I hear he's as brave
as a lion," said Sampson
the stoat.

"I hear he's as purple as a plum," chirped William, a wood warbler. All the animals wanted to meet Blaze, even the bigger ones like Daisy, a gentle doe.

I hear he's as strong as a stag!

Chirp!

William, Sampson and Daisy tried to think
of ways to tempt Blaze down from the trees.
"I love nibbling bark," said Daisy. So she
put out some of her favourite bark,
and waited.

From the treetops, Blaze could see what was happening, but he was not interested in the bark.

"Do they really think some dry bark will tempt me out of my tree?" he laughed.

Sampson did not want to give up any of his favourite food. Instead he put out some flowers that he spotted growing nearby.

"All butterflies love drinking nectar from flowers," he said.

But Sampson did not know that purple emperors were not like ordinary butterflies and did not drink nectar.

Nectar?
No thank you!

69

William had heard stories that purple emperor butterflies helped to keep the forest clean by feeding on animal droppings from the forest floor. But when he suggested that they put out some of their droppings, Daisy and Sampson wrinkled their noses.

"I'm not doing that!" said Daisy.
"Me neither!" said Sampson.
So the animals called another meeting
to work out a new plan.

Ewww!

But William was right. Sometimes Blaze did fly down to the forest floor to feed on droppings. He needed the salt in them to stay healthy.

Blaze now thought he saw his chance to do just that, as Sampson and Daisy were so busy talking. But just as he landed, William spotted Blaze and hopped towards him.

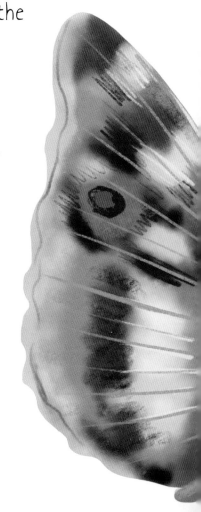

Shoo!
Go away!

73

When William had almost reached him, Blaze flew off in a flash of purple. Then William saw something amazing... there in a bush was another beautiful butterfly like Blaze, but this one was a deep chestnut brown.

Hello little
warbler, can I
help you?

The butterfly's name was Bella. William told
her about the plans to tempt Blaze, but how
no one would listen to his idea. So Bella and
William made a plan of their own.

Eventually, Sampson noticed that William
was missing, and looked around for him.
"Quick, hide!" William said to Bella.
"Who were you talking to?" asked Sampson.

Let me
explain.

Suddenly Bella fluttered in front of everyone.

"I will help you to meet Blaze," she said. "But you all need to hide while I stay here."

Flutter!

From his treetop, Blaze looked down and saw a beautiful butterfly. He had caught sight of her just before flying away from the pesky warbler. Blaze really wanted to meet her, and he forgot all about hiding from everyone. He swooped and twirled through the air, and his purple wings shimmered in the sunlight. He spiralled lower and lower in a magnificent dance.

"Wow!" whispered the animals who were peeping through the leaves.

"Surprise!" shouted Daisy and Sampson as Blaze landed.

"You tricked me!" said Blaze. But he did not mind any more. If Bella was friends with these animals then he could be, too. The butterflies took off, gracefully gliding up to the top of the biggest oak tree. It was a dazzling display the animals would never forget.

"Those are the most magnificent butterflies I have ever seen!" beamed William.

The Copycat Chameleon

Illustrated by Veronica Montoya

Cedric the chameleon lived in a beautiful rainforest on an island called Madagascar. Some very special animals and plants lived on Cedric's island. They were so special, they were not found anywhere else in the world. Cedric wished he was special, too, but he did not feel it.

One morning, Cedric was trying to catch a tasty bug for breakfast. "If I could just reach a little further," he said.

Zip! Out flashed his tongue...

...but something blue shot through the trees and knocked him sideways.

"Hey, you just stopped me catching breakfast!" moaned Cedric.

"Oh, I'm sorry," said the coua bird, who was called Carole.

Carole showed Cedric the wonderful nest she was building.

"I wish I could build something as amazing as that," said Cedric.

You are so clever.

Cedric wished he was just like Carole. He closed his eyes and imagined he was as blue as the sparkling ocean.

When Cedric opened his eyes he had turned a beautiful blue!

Cedric still didn't feel special even though he was a beautiful blue. He spotted a curious beetle behaving strangely a few trees away, which took his mind off things.

Wow!

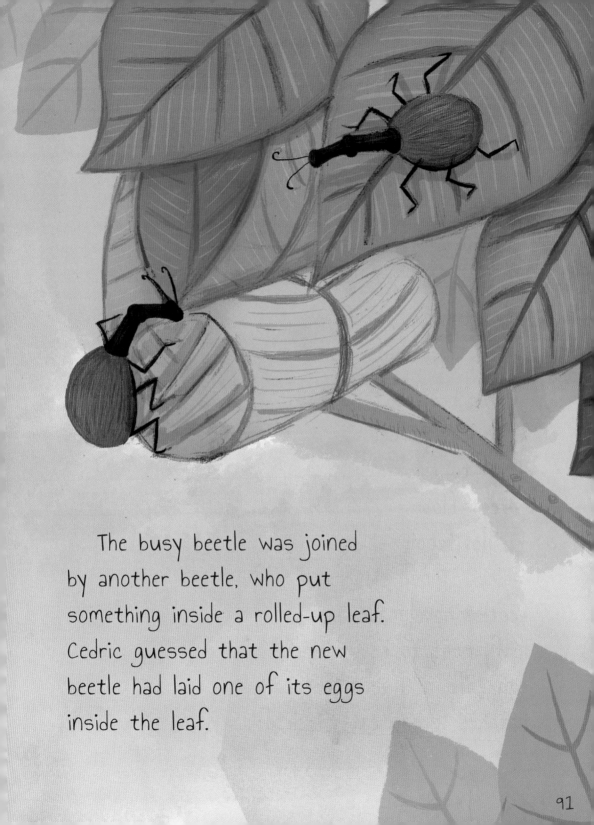

The busy beetle was joined
by another beetle, who put
something inside a rolled-up leaf.
Cedric guessed that the new
beetle had laid one of its eggs
inside the leaf.

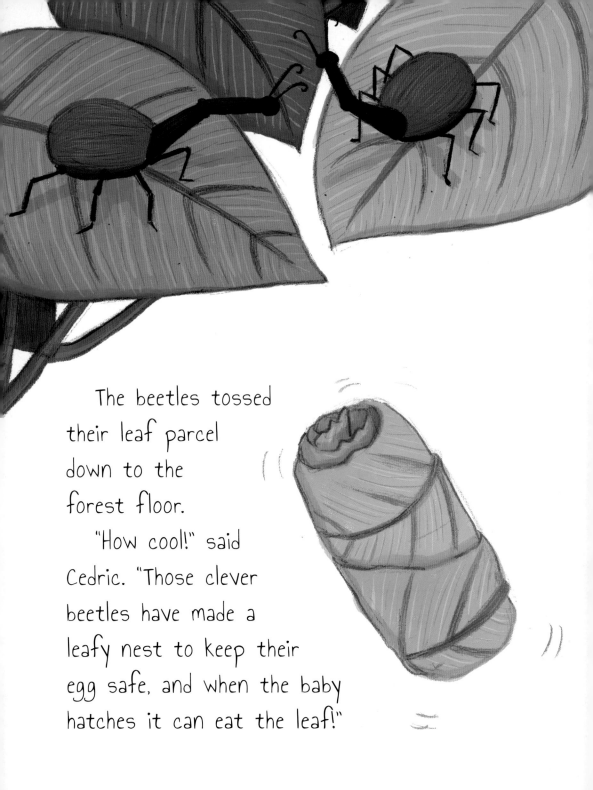

The beetles tossed
their leaf parcel
down to the
forest floor.

"How cool!" said
Cedric. "Those clever
beetles have made a
leafy nest to keep their
egg safe, and when the baby
hatches it can eat the leaf!"

Cedric now
wished he was special like
the beetles. He closed his eyes
and imagined he was as red as a
juicy strawberry, just like them.
And when he opened his eyes he
had turned a deep red.

But Cedric still did not feel special. He hoped he would feel better soon.

Click-clack! Click-clack!

"What's that?" wondered Cedric. "I've not heard that sound in the forest before."

A tenrec, whose name was Tamby, was
clicking her tongue to call her mother.

"I can make other sounds, too," said Tamby,
and she rubbed her spines together.
Scritch-scratch! went her spines.

Scritch-scratch!

"That's so cool that you can make all of those sounds," said Cedric.

"My mother's here so I must go now," replied Tamby. "Maybe I'll teach you how to make them next time."

Cedric now wished he was special like Tamby. He closed his eyes and imagined he was as yellow as a fluffy bee, just like Tamby. And when he opened his eyes he had turned a golden yellow.

But Cedric still did not feel special. He went all over the forest speaking to other animals, asking what made them so special. A ruffed lemur called Ricardo helped magnificent palm trees to grow by spreading seeds around the forest.

I eat the fruit, then the seeds come out in my poo!

A mantella frog called Marina was a super climber with sticky fingers and toes.

Lio, a leaf-nosed snake, could disguise himself as a leafy twig and wait for his dinner to walk by.

Cedric wanted to be special
like Ricardo so he turned himself
as black as the night sky.

Then Cedric wanted
to be like Marina, so he
turned himself orange like
the delicious fruit.

He still wasn't happy, so he turned himself
as brown as a tree trunk, just like Lio.

But do you think any
of these changes made
Cedric feel special?

"I'm never going to feel special," sighed Cedric, and he turned himself green again so he could hide among the leaves. He hardly noticed when another chameleon spoke to him.

Hello! My name is Clementine.

"Are you speaking to me?" asked Cedric. He did not believe that such a pretty chameleon had noticed him. But Clementine had often seen Cedric and wanted to get to know him.

Cedric and Clementine started spending time together, and Cedric began to feel special.

"You don't need to copy anyone," smiled Clementine.

You are special to me just as you are.

And one other thing
made Cedric happy.

He was going to be a daddy! Soon he
would have his own family to care for.
What could be more special than that?

The Naughty Shrew

Illustrated by Annie Wilkinson

Autumn was the time when many young forest animals left their homes, and the forest was full of nuts, berries and fungi. Animals were fattening up or storing food for winter, when there was less to eat.

Sven the shrew lived in a nest with his brothers and sisters. Soon they would all leave home, but first Sven wanted to get up to some mischief.

ZZZZZ

Sven was always getting up to mischief.
This particular morning, when he was
supposed to be napping with his family, he
crept outside in search of an acorn.

Sven pushed the acorn hard into the nest and **SMACK!** All the young shrews woke up.

"What was that?" said Sven's little sister.

"Danger!" shouted their mother. "We must move nests!"

Naughty Sven did not tell them about the acorn. So all of the young shrews followed their mother out into the cool morning, holding on to each other's tails.

"Stay close to me," said mother shrew.

Soon they met a prickly hedgehog, whose name was Hettie. She had been hunting for juicy worms and slugs all night, so was looking for a cosy place to curl up and sleep.

"Where are you all off to?" yawned Hettie.

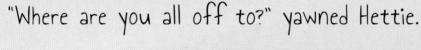

113

"Hurry up Sven!" called his mother.

Sven was dragging his paws as he was looking for something naughty to do next.

Splat! A blackberry exploded everywhere.

"Eww!" cried Sven's sister, as Sven giggled beside her.

SPLAT!

"What have you done?" asked mother shrew. "You are so naughty Sven!" She hurried them away before they woke the dormouse, to whom the blackberries belonged.

Up ahead, Sven spotted a red squirrel.
She was burying something and kept looking
around to see if anyone was watching. When
she spotted the shrews she darted up a tree.

"What did that squirrel bury?" Sven asked his mother.

"That's none of our business," she replied. But Sven was not so sure and was thinking of mischievous things.

It felt like they
had been walking forever.
   "How far is our new
home?" asked one of Sven's
brothers.
   "It's just past that tree
with the twirling seeds,"
said mother shrew.

But Sven was not listening, as he was thinking of what mischief he could get up to next. He let go of his sister's tail and slipped away into the forest.

Sven headed back to where he had spotted the secretive squirrel. He scraped away the leaves to find... an acorn!

"Is that all?" Sven laughed. Shrews did not eat acorns like squirrels. But Sven still thought it would be funny to dig up all the squirrel's acorns and hide them somewhere else.

Hiding the squirrel's acorns gave Sven an idea of the next naughty thing he could do. He made his way back to the home of the dormouse, whose name was Denis.

All of the blackberries and hazelnuts were still there, as Denis was fast asleep. One at a time, Sven quietly piled Denis' treats on a leaf and then dragged them away.

It did not take Sven long to find the next animal to play a joke on. He heard Hettie's spikes rustling in the leaves.

"Excuse me," Sven said bravely.

I've seen a cosy spot for you to sleep.

"Please tell me where it is," said Hettie.

Sven sent Hettie towards the stream. But do you think he had really seen a cosy spot for her?

125

Sven had caused a lot of trouble this time!
He ran through the forest. Not far behind him
was a furious Hettie.

She was followed by an angry Denis.

"Where have you hidden my blackberries and hazelnuts?" he cried. Then Denis was followed by a furious red squirrel, named Sylvie.

Stop, you naughty shrew!

Sven reached his new nest, and dived in.
But where were his brothers and sisters?

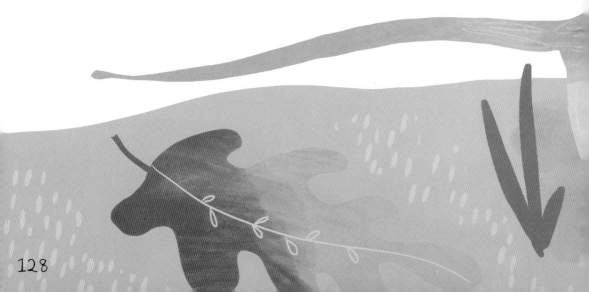

"They have left home," said Sven's mother. "But you will stay with me until you can respect other animals in the forest."

Sven realized it was time to stop being naughty. He wanted to prove that he could be good, and he said sorry to all the animals he had upset. Just a week later, he left home.

Bye Mum!

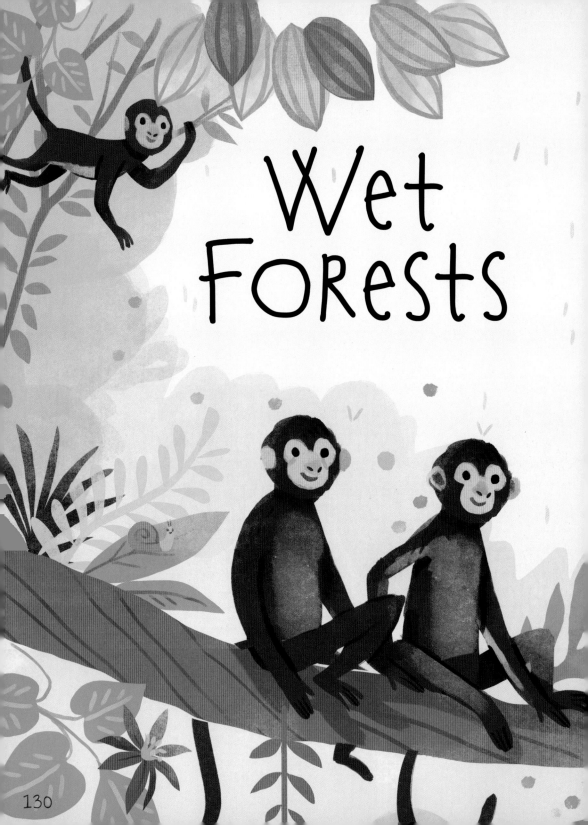

Wet Forests

Some forests are hot and humid, and
it rains almost every day. We call them
rainforests, or jungles. These special places
are home to amazing animals that are found
nowhere else in the world. Read on to hear
some stories from just a few of them.

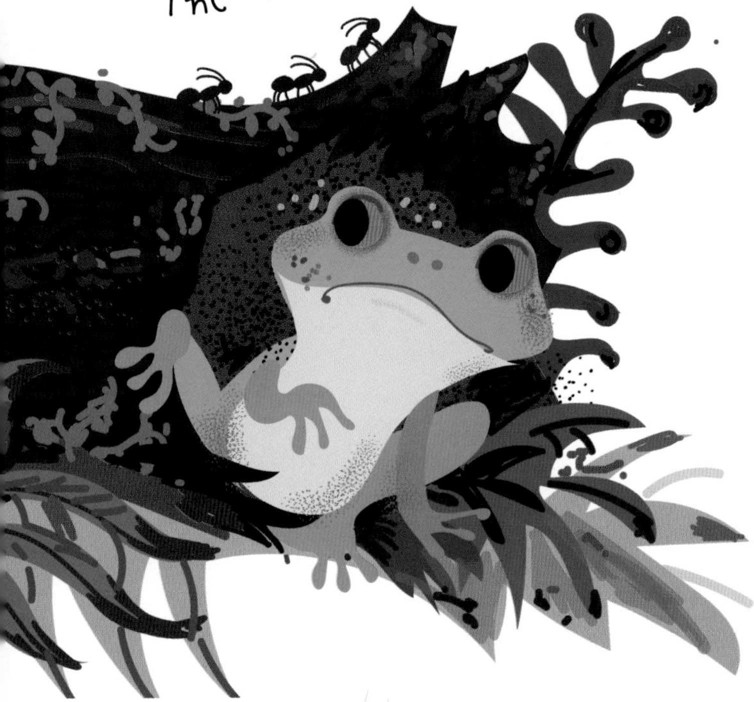

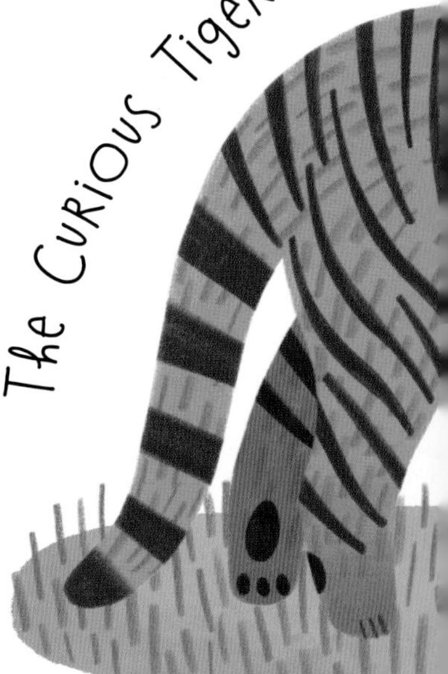

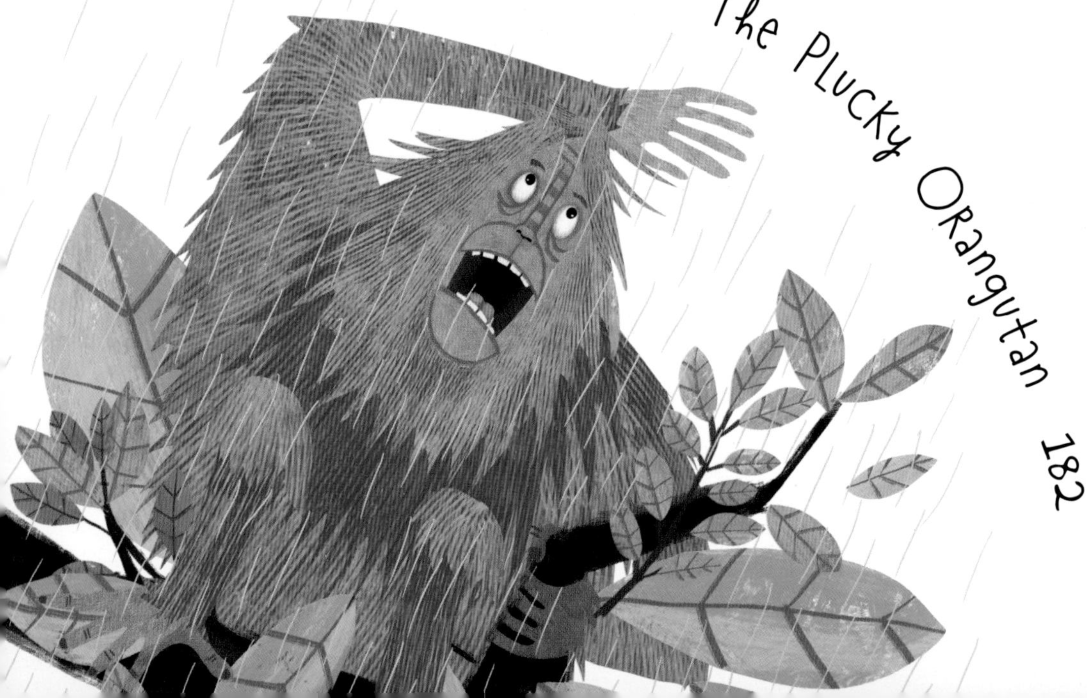

The Timid Frog

Illustrated by Amanda Enright

All the nocturnal animals were waking up for the evening.

"Eek! What's that?" Fae the giant tree frog was afraid of everything that moved.

Now that she was no longer a tadpole and had grown up, it was time for Fae to leave her forest pool. Her brothers and sisters had already left to live in the trees.

It felt strange standing on land with her new legs for the first time.

Nervously Fae hopped across the leafy forest floor onto a fallen branch.

"Hey, watch out!" said Lluka a leaf-tailed gecko. "You're hopping on my tail!"

S...s...sorry, your tail looks just like a leaf.

Fae asked Lluka if she had seen her family. "I saw some frogs hopping that way," said Lluka. "But watch out for a wild pig who eats frogs like you."

Honk!   Squeal!

Suddenly there was loud honk! and squeal!
Fae remembered Lluka's warning and darted
inside a hollow log just in time. A wild pig
charged past, making Fae tremble.

When the pig had gone, Fae crept out of her hiding place. She wished that she could return to her forest pool where she felt safe and happy.

"He...lllooooo!" echoed the log behind Fae. She sprang round to face whatever had been hiding in the log with her.

"Who's there?" she asked shyly.

"Sorry I startled you. I'm Birrani, a bandicoot."

Fae and Birrani climbed onto the log and laughed at what a scaredy-cat Fae had been.

"I saw some frogs climbing that tree," said Birrani.

Fae was hopeful that she would soon see her family.

Fae stood at the bottom of a huge tree that seemed to go on forever. It had been raining and the trunk was wet and slippery.

"How can I climb that?" she whispered to herself.

Fae took a deep breath and leapt onto the trunk.

My toes stick like glue to the tree!

Climbing the tree was
easier than she thought.

But Fae was not alone in the tree...

ZZZZZZZZZZZZZZZZZZZZZZZZZZ

Above Fae, and blocking her path, was a huge, sleeping frilled lizard! Fae did not know if the lizard was friendly, but she wasn't hanging around to find out!

There was no way round the snoozing lizard so Fae would have to do a huge hop over it.

"One, two, three," she counted, and then...

...Fae leapt magnificently over the lizard, but landed right in front of a dozing green tree python!

"Argh!" gasped Fae. Her big brother had often frightened her with stories of snakes that gobbled up frogs. Luckily, this snake had just eaten and was fast asleep. But Fae certainly didn't want to wake him!

Please don't wake up!

ZzzZzz

"Pssst," whispered a voice that made Fae jump. She looked up. Two bright eyes belonging to a spotted cuscus stared from between the leaves. "Hop up the vine," the cuscus said.

"Thanks," replied Fae. She was glad to leave the snake behind.

"I'm Calen," said the cuscus.

Calen said that some frogs had passed him just yesterday, and told Fae to follow him.

But Calen was not the quickest animal in the rainforest! He climbed so slowly that Fae could not wait a minute longer. She sprang over Calen, zipped along the branch and bashed into...

...Freya the flying fox.

"Who do we have here?" asked Freya between mouthfuls of fruit.

"Don't worry," gulped Fae. "I'm not hanging around," and she hopped past Freya as fast as she could.

Next Fae met Soo the sugar glider who had some bad news.

"Some green-eyed tree frogs live in THIS tree, but a family of giant tree frogs live over in THAT tree," said Soo.

Fae had climbed the wrong tree!
"I can't jump to that tree from
here," she wept.
"I have an idea," replied Soo.

Aaaaaargh!

Soo told Fae to climb onto her back. Fae clung on tight and screamed as they glided through the air. **Thwack!**

They had made it! Fae's brothers and
sisters were there and she could not wait
to tell them all about her journey.

"I can't believe how brave you are now,"
said Flyn, Fae's eldest brother.

Fae smiled at Flyn and said,
"Yes, I am brave!"

The CURIOUS TigeR

Illustrated by Jean Claude

One evening, a mother tiger was taking her cubs, Tejas and Tara, through the forest. She wanted to teach them which animals to hunt for food. Tejas was always asking questions. But his mother did not mind, because being curious helped Tejas learn.

"Will we catch any animals?" he asked.

"Not this evening because our tummies are full," said his mother.

Silently they crept through the mangrove forest and soon they spotted an animal snuffling in the wet mud.

"That's a wild boar," whispered mother tiger. "Wild boars are very tasty!"

Mother tiger and Tara carried on, but Tejas stayed behind. "Excuse me," he said to the boar, who was called Bristi, "what do you eat?"

Bristi looked fearfully at the tiger cub, but could see that his tummy was full.

I like eating roots and shoots.

"Where were you?" scolded Tara, as Tejas caught up with his family.

"Sssh!" said their mother. She was watching a monkey up in the trees. Tejas' mother told him it was a macaque, which is delicious.

Once again Tejas stayed behind. He asked
the macaque, who was called Mitu, "What are
you eating?"

"I'm snacking on some fruit before bedtime,"
replied Mitu. She felt perfectly safe high up in
her tree.

"Try to keep up!" said Tara, as Tejas joined his family again.

"Quiet now!" said mother tiger. "Can you see a spotted deer? Tigers love eating deer."

Tejas was bursting with questions to ask the deer, so he hung back. The deer could tell that Tejas was not hungry. He said his name was Divum and that he liked to nibble leaves.

Tejas had learnt so much from asking questions.

"I have something else to show you," said mother tiger.

She took the cubs to a part of the forest where there were no longer any trees. Tejas could not believe what he saw.

"They have been chopped down," replied his mother.

"But why?" asked Tejas.

"To make room for other things," said his mother.

Mother tiger continued, "Because there is no forest here anymore, there are no wild boars, no macaques and no spotted deer, as there is no food or shelter for them."

"We can't stay here either, can we?" said Tejas. "There are no animals for us to eat."

It was time to head back into the forest.

Tejas needed cheering up, so mother tiger took the cubs swimming. All tigers love swimming!

"Race you to the river," shouted Tara, who was almost there already.

SPLASH!

In the river Tejas met an otter. He could not stop himself asking another question.

"What do you like to eat?"

"I especially like eating crabs," replied Oditi the otter, who was a much better swimmer than any tiger.

"If otters eat crabs, what do crabs eat?" Tejas asked his mother.

"Why don't you ask one?" replied mother tiger. So Tejas swam over to the soggy, muddy bank to find some crabs.

The crabs sank back into the mud when they saw Tejas. But Choti, a brave fiddler crab, nipped Tejas' paw and said,

I nibble on dead animals, which keeps the river clean.

There were so many animals living in the mangrove forest and word quickly spread that a curious tiger cub was asking questions.

Animals grew bold and came out of their hiding places. A crocodile snapped that it liked to eat snakes, a snake hissed that it ate birds, and a bird quacked that it snacked on crabs.

Soon it was time for the tigers to head back to their favourite spot under a mangrove tree to sleep.

Tejas did a big tigery shake to dry off. He was bubbling with excitement all the way home and could not stop chatting, telling Tara everything he had learnt that evening.

Tejas didn't want a story for bedtime. He wanted to hear more about his forest.

"By asking questions I found out that some animals eat plants. And that others, like us tigers, eat animals," he told his mother. "Is there anything that hunts tigers?"

"I'll answer that question when you're a little older," said mother tiger. "But learning all about the forest will help to keep you safe. Goodnight, Tejas."

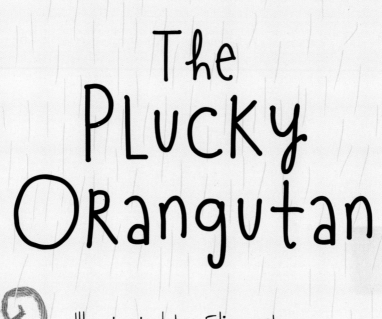

The PLUCKY ORangutan

Illustrated by Elissambura

Oma the orangutan wanted to be good at everything. She loved trying new things.

Every waking hour, when she was not eating or napping, she loved doing challenges.

One day, Oma's friend Amir challenged her to build the best tree nest.

"It will be the cosiest nest any orangutan has ever made!" said Oma, as she gathered branches with the biggest, softest leaves to line her new nest.

But...

Whoosh... a rain cloud burst overhead! Rain flooded into Oma's nest and quickly soaked the leaves, and Oma.

"I wish you would GO AWAY!" Oma shouted at the rain. "Look at my soggy bottom! I'm not the best at building a cosy nest."

"Why don't you try building a nest in the fastest time instead?" said Amir, as he sheltered under a giant leaf.

Word spread about Oma's next challenge and when the rain stopped, she was ready to begin. Vina, who was the fastest nest-builder many years ago, counted Oma down...

"One, two, three, orangutan-go!"
The sounds of bend... snap, bend... snap
echoed around the forest as Oma whipped
branches off the trees. But the branches
were wet and slimy, and many slipped out
of her hands.

"Time's up!" shouted Vina.
"Stop what you're doing."
   Oma did not feel confident
with this challenge either.
   "Can you stand up in
your nest?" shouted one of
the watching orangutans.

Oma nervously stepped in.
But... her nest was not very
strong!

"I'm not the best at building
nests in super-quick time
either," said Oma sadly.

Amir suggested that for
Oma's next challenge, she could
try building the highest nest.

Oma bravely climbed the tallest tree she could find. She could see for miles!

"It's windy up here!" she nervously shouted down. But she would not give up the challenge.

"I CAN do this," she told herself.

Amir was not so sure about the view when he joined Oma.

"Look, the rain clouds are coming back!"

Oma and Amir scrambled down just in time, as heavy rain washed Oma's nest away.

"My idea to build a nest that high was not so great!" said Amir, as leaves and branches fell on Oma's head.

Oma did not believe Amir. The two friends
carried on arguing and were getting wetter
and wetter.

"I challenge you to prove that plants need
the rain," said Oma. "Let's have a competition!"

When it stopped raining, Amir was ready to take up Oma's challenge. Vina volunteered to judge the competition and gave each of them a young tree to plant.

It did not take Amir long to find the
perfect spot to plant his tree.

"Here my sapling will have shelter, light, and
the rain will drip off that leaf and water it,"
he said.

Oma found it much harder to find a spot
for her tree. But eventually she found a dry
tree hollow that did not have any animals in.

After a week it was time to check on the young trees. First they all went to Amir's sapling.

"I don't believe it!" Amir beamed. "My sapling has grown five more leaves!"

Then they went to look at Oma's sapling.
Sadly, her small tree had not grown any
more leaves.

But Oma was still hopeful. "Perhaps it's a
slow starter, like me!" she said.

After two weeks it was time for the final
check. Amir's sapling had grown tall and strong.

"I knew the rain would help my tree to
grow!" boasted Amir.

But Oma's sapling looked very sorry for
itself. It had wilted and withered. This was
another challenge that Oma had not won.

"Now do you believe me?" asked Amir.

Oma was sad. "I'm not the best at building nests or growing a tree."

"But you are the best at something," said Vina.

Oma could not think of anything she was good at.

"Everytime something went wrong, you kept trying and you never gave up," smiled Vina. "You are the best at trying your best."

"And the best at making people laugh!" added Amir.

The Fussy Gorilla

Illustrated by Sophia Touliatou

The one thing that Gabi the gorilla loved eating more than anything else was... ants! Gorillas do eat ants from time to time, but the problem was that Gabi ate ants all of the time. Breakfast, lunch and dinner was always ants! Her mother was always saying to her, "You eat so many ants that soon you'll look like an ant!"

It was a rainy day in the rainforest
and Gabi was having fun with her friends.
"Let's have a race," she shouted. And
in a flash she was off... Whoosh!

She skidded round bends, zipped past surprised gorillas and jumped over fallen branches. Gabi was going so fast that she did not have time to stop, and ran straight into...

Whoosh!

...an ant nest!

"Are you okay Gabi?" asked her friend Kwame when he caught up. But Gabi was more than fine, as what lives in an ant nest? Ants, of course!

This was the perfect start to Gabi's day. By the time everyone caught up, Gabi had eaten hundreds of ants. She was beginning to feel full!

"What shall we do now?" asked Kwame.

But Gabi was up a tree and onto the next game already. "Last one to the crooked tree is a squashed banana!" Gabi shouted.

The young gorillas raced towards the crooked tree. They all tried to catch up with Gabi, who was in the lead, and she would have won, except...

As Gabi stepped on a branch, she spotted something scuttling under the bark.

"I need to investigate this," she said, and carefully peeled off some bark.

Delicious! Gabi had found some more tasty ants. This day kept getting better! By the time her friends had joined her, Gabi had eaten most of the ants and was feeling very full and sleepy.

But Gabi would never turn down
a game of hide-and-seek.
   "Three, two, one... coming!"
shouted Kwame.

It did not take Kwame very long to find
Jamila. Now it was just Gabi to track down.

Zzzzzz!

But where was she?
It was getting late and
they had to get back to their
troop for lunch.

Zzzzzz! "Did you hear that?" said Jamila.
What a surprise. There was Gabi, and she was
fast asleep in a pile of leaves!

Sagan was a silverback gorilla, and the leader of Gabi's troop. He was cross when he heard how Gabi had fallen asleep after eating so many ants and made her friends late back. He went to talk to her.

"Look where eating all those ants has got you," said Sagan. "Eating so many is not good for you or the forest."

I am going to teach you about our rainforest.

Sagan showed Gabi a tree covered in berries. "Gorillas like berries," he said.

Gabi nibbled a few. They tasted okay, but they were not ants!

The berries contain seeds. We eat the berries, then the seeds come out in our poo.

"We help to scatter the seeds that will grow into new trees," said Sagan.

223

Next they explored the forest floor. Sagan showed Gabi some tasty flowers that gorillas sometimes ate. Gabi nibbled a flower, and it tasted nice, but it was still not an ant.

"Just like berries, when we eat flowers we help to scatter the flower seeds in our poo," said Sagan. Gabi liked the good things gorillas did for the forest.

Lastly, Sagan took Gabi to a place she knew very well... back to her mother and all her friends.

"Most of all, gorillas love eating leaves, shoots and stems!"

"These plants grow so quickly that the forest would be overgrown if we did not eat them," said Sagan.

Gabi could not wait to try a leaf.

We are the gardeners of the forest.

Gabi felt proud to hear about all
the good things gorillas did for their
rainforest. She wanted to help the
forest and grow big and strong, too.

"I will try to eat lots of different
things in future," said Gabi. "With
maybe just a few ants" she added
with a grin.

The Storyteller Sloth

Illustrated by Kathryn Selbert

Salvidor Sloth's two favourite things were hanging out on his special branch and telling stories about the rainforest.

One rainy day, Sophia and Felipe the spider monkeys turned up at Salvidor's branch and asked him to tell them a story. Salvidor was very pleased.

He looked at their eager faces and
had an idea for an exciting story.

233

Sofia wanted a front row
seat and settled close
to Salvidor. He
cleared his throat
and began.

Once upon a
time there was a
little spider monkey
called Camila...

"...Like all spider monkeys,
Camila's brothers and sisters were
experts at climbing trees, using their
long tails as extra arms to grip onto
branches."

"I can do that!" Sofia interrupted.

235

Word began to spread about Salvidor's story, and other animals came to listen. The spider monkeys were soon joined by some squirrel monkeys. The rain splish sploshed on the branch.

Splish splosh!

Salvidor continued, "...But Camila wasn't like other spider monkeys because she had an extra long tail. Her tail was so long that it was always getting in the way. So Camila's friends called her 'Clumsy Camila.'"

Word spread further through the rainforest, and next a green iguana came to listen. The spider monkeys and the squirrel monkeys shuffled along the branch to make room for him. The rain drummed on their heads.

Soon, there were so many animals crowded onto the branch that Salvidor had to speak up.

"One day, as Camila slept, a big snake slithered along the tree..."

Eek!
Oh no!

Then, just as Salvidor was getting
to the exciting part of his story, there
was an almighty crack! And **whoosh!**
All the animals went flying.

241

A wet Salvidor fell down and down. He swooshed past Juan, a snoozing jaguar, who opened one eye lazily.

Hey! What is going on?

Not far behind Salvidor, five dripping spider monkeys, four squishy squirrel monkeys and one damp green iguana all swooshed past Juan, too.

243

Plop! Salvidor dropped onto the forest floor at the top of a muddy slope. He nearly landed on Gabriel, a giant armadillo. Luckily, Gabriel was snoring so loudly, he didn't notice Salvidor.

ZZZZZ!

One by one, five soggy spider monkeys, four sopping squirrel monkeys and one dripping green iguana also plopped onto the muddy slope in front of Gabriel. They didn't wake him up either!

Salvidor tried to stand but he lost his footing on the squelchy, muddy slope and tumbled past Pia the peccary. He was covered in mud now and didn't look much like a sloth anymore.

"Watch out!" Sofia screamed at Pia, as the spider monkeys, squirrel monkeys and green iguana followed Salvidor down the oozy, muddy slope.

Salvidor had to think fast. As he shot between two trees he flung out his arms, dug in his claws and held on tight.

"Fall into me!" he shouted. A few seconds later, one by one, the five spider monkeys, four squirrel monkeys and the green iguana fell into his soft, muddy body.

The rain washed the mud off the animals as they began to climb up through the layers of the rainforest.

"See you soon," Sofia yelled to Salvidor as she leapt on ahead.

By the time Salvidor had joined the other animals in the treetops, they had found him a new sturdy branch. Salvidor was pleased with his new home and was ready to finish his story...

"Camila woke with a start. As she spun round to see what was behind her, her long tail whipped round too. The snake thought her tail was an even bigger snake, and slithered off fast."

"Tell another story, please," begged Sofia.
But Salvidor had had enough of telling stories
for a while. He was now going to do his
second favourite thing, which was sleeping.

Zzzzz

Snowy
Forests

A forest is a magical place when covered by a blanket of snow. Animals that make their homes here might have thick fur or feathers to keep warm. Others might sleep in cosy dens until the wintery weather has gone. Read on for some super snowy adventures.

The Bossy Owl

Illustrated by David Creighton-Pester

Travis the tawny owl was the best hunter in his forest. He had super-sharp hearing, incredible eyesight, spiky talons and powerful wings. Finding and catching prey was easy for him, even on snowy winter evenings.

Woo hoo!

"I can catch anything that moves!" he
boasted to his mate Bonnie, who was perched
in their nest. Then off Travis flew on his
evening hunt.

Travis flew silently
between trees, listening for
prey. He heard the tiny squeak
of a mouse under the snow,
and in a flash swooped
down to catch it.

Hey! How dare you hunt in MY forest!

But just before he could reach the mouse, another owl, whose name was Tom, swooped in and took it! Travis hovered furiously above Tom, shouting at him.

Tom flew off without replying.

"How rude!" said Travis. But there was hunting to be done, so Travis took to the air again.

Suddenly, Travis heard the scurrying of a vole below. He was just about to swoop down on it, when he saw that Tom had got there first again. Travis was furious, but Tom flew off just like before.

Squeak!

Then Travis spotted a juicy worm poking its head out of the snowy soil. He prepared to swoop down on it faster than ever before.

This time I'll be ready for you!

But WHOOSH!
Tom was there again,
just pulling the worm
out of the soil.

Travis had no time to lose.
He flew down to claim
the worm!

Quickly Travis grabbed the other end of the worm. He pulled one end and Tom pulled the other. Travis puffed up his feathers.

"You cannot hunt in MY forest!" he said to Tom. This time Tom did reply.

"It's not YOUR forest!"

Eeek!

But the second both Travis and Tom opened
their beaks to speak, the lucky worm fell out!

The worm knew better than to hang around, and quickly slipped away. It could still hear Travis and Tom arguing.

Just then, a badger came to see what all the noise was about.

Shush! I may be awake, but other animals are sleeping!

The owls could not agree, so Tom flew off one way in a bad mood, and Travis flew the other way in a huff.

The next evening, Travis said goodbye to
Bonnie as usual and set off to hunt. But
this time he flew to his secret hunting
ground, a spot that no other owls
knew about.

Tom had also set off to hunt
again. And both he and Travis
were flying towards each other
to the same spot in the forest!

As Travis flew east, Tom flew west. Closer and closer they flew. Until...

"Woah!" shouted Travis, as both owls flapped to a halt in mid-air. They looked at each other in surprise, then looked below and got an even bigger shock.

275

Travis tried to listen for prey, but the traffic was so noisy he could not hear any animals.

I can't hunt in this noise.

Tom also tried to listen for prey, but the traffic was too noisy for him. "I can't hunt in this noise either," he said. Both owls went home hungry.

The next evening, instead of arguing, Travis and Tom tried to work things out. The forest was big enough for both of them after all.

Travis drew in the snow with a stick. "As this is **our** forest, I will hunt on **this** side of the road," he said.

Tom then took the stick
and drew in the snow.

And I will hunt
on THIS side of
the road.

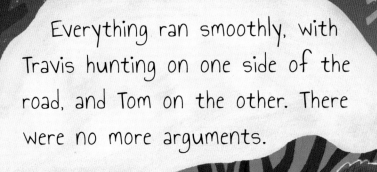

Everything ran smoothly, with Travis hunting on one side of the road, and Tom on the other. There were no more arguments.

They caught lots of mice, voles and worms and took them back to their mates.

"It's much better to work things out than to argue," Travis said happily to Bonnie.

The Hungry Panda

Illustrated by
Paul Nicholls

Ping lived with his mother in a bamboo forest in the mountains. Just like all giant pandas, he loved eating bamboo. When he was not eating, Ping's next favourite thing was sleeping. He loved these two things so much that it was hard to make him do anything else.

Crunch munch!

And sometimes, Ping's mother asked him to do other things!

This wintery morning was one of those times.

"It's too cold for us here," said Ping's mother. "We need to move down the mountain."

But Ping did not answer because he was too busy eating.

"Did you hear me?" asked mother panda.
"Yes Mum," Ping said between bites. These juicy bamboo shoots were too good to leave. What was Mother thinking leaving all of this behind?

Crunch munch!

Mother panda led the way
through the forest, down the
mountain. But the bamboo
they passed was too tempting
for Ping and he kept stopping
to nibble along the way.

Yum!

Keep up
Ping!

The more Ping nibbled, the fuller he felt and the slower he trudged through the snow. Mother was getting further and further ahead.

Zzzzzz!

"I'll just have a nap, then I'll catch up," said Ping. But suddenly...

"Owww!" howled Ping. "Who is throwing snowballs at me? I was dreaming I had all the bamboo I could ever eat."

"Hi! I'm Genji," said a golden
monkey. "What are you doing all
on your own in the forest?"

When Ping realized that he had lost his
mother, he started to cry.

"Look!" said Genji pointing at some large paw prints in the snow. "They are so huge they must belong to your mother."

Let's follow them.

But once again, Ping found the bamboo too tempting and he gobbled leaves and shoots along the way. Genji was getting further ahead.

"I'll just have forty winks, then I'll catch up," said Ping.

"Hey, what are you doing?" said Ping as he was woken by someone trying to steal some bamboo from his paws.

"I'm sorry," said Ru the red panda. "It just looked so tasty."

Ping told Ru how he and his friend Genji had been following his mother's paw prints.

"But now Genji has gone and new snow has covered the paw prints so they are gone, too!" he wailed.

Ru had an idea. "ALL kinds of pandas like climbing trees!" But Ping wasn't so sure.

We may spot your mother from high up in the trees.

296

"I've never done this before," said Ping nervously as they climbed up the tallest tree. But it was worth it, as from the top they could see for miles.

That's her!
That's my
mum!

Ping shouted as he spotted
a smudge of black against the
white snow.

"It could be anything," said Ru.
But Ping knew it was his mother.

Bumpety bump!

Ping slid down the snowy tree.

"Thanks for your help Ru," he shouted. This time he was not going to eat or sleep until he reached his mother.

But as he trotted along, Ping slipped on a pile of leafy bamboo shoots that he had been eating before he met Ru. The shoots were like a sledge and carried him down the mountain slope.

SWISH!

"Wheee!" Ping was enjoying the ride. He crashed through the bamboo forest and only came to a stop when he thumped into something warm, soft and furry. "Mother!" Ping shouted.

Ping looked around. "I don't understand.
Where has our forest gone?" asked Ping.
"It's on the other side of this road,"
said mother panda.

How do
we get to the
other side?

Then Ping noticed what looked like a
tunnel beneath the road, and went to look.
"Mind the road," called his mother.

Ping had spotted a forest pathway that
went under the road. Mother panda led the
way through.

"We'll be warm down here for the winter,"
she said. "When the spring comes, we'll go
back up the mountain."

Can you guess the first thing Ping
wanted to do in his new forest home?

Of course...
eat bamboo, and
then have a sleep!

The Adventurous Wolf

Illustrated by Fabrizio di Baldo

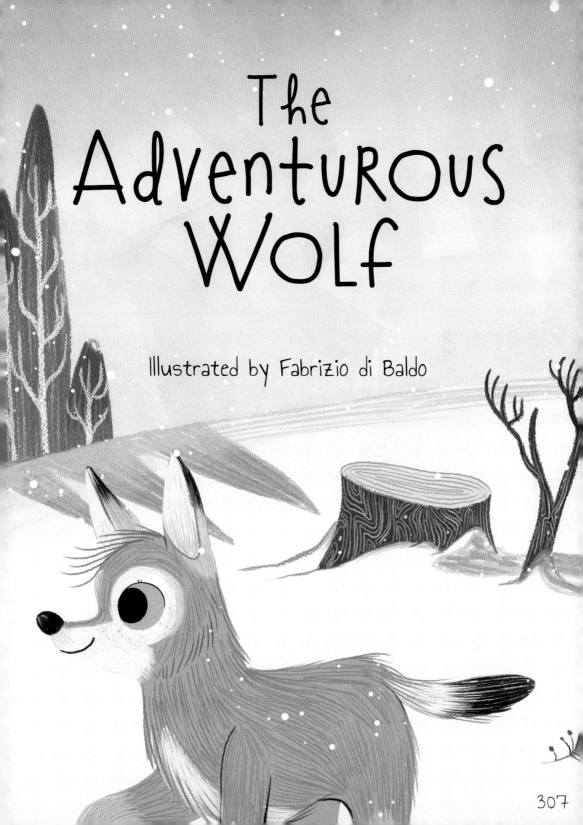

Galina was the smallest grey wolf cub in her pack. She could not wait to grow up and have adventures. The only place she had known since she was born was her den.

However, now they were getting bigger, Galina and her brothers and sisters went outside more.

It was winter, and everything in the forest was covered in magical, white snow.

One evening, all of the pack
except Galina left to go on a
hunt. Even her brothers and
sisters went this time.

As the smallest, Galina had to stay behind. But she wanted an adventure and was not going to wait for her pack to return.

I will have an adventure of my own!

Walking in the snow with her large paws was easier than Galina thought. But it was so cold! She was glad she had a thick fur coat to keep her warm. Suddenly, a loud voice called out to Galina.

Crunch!

Hello, little one! My name is Evgeni, I am an elk.

Galina stared at this strange new animal. He looked like he had trees growing out of his head!

"Wolves hunt elks," said Galina, but she wanted friends with Evgeni.
"What exciting things do you do in the forest?" asked Galina curiously.

"I find tasty water plants to snack on in the river," replied Evgeni. With that, he stepped into the freezing water and set off swimming.

Galina crouched down, took a deep breath, and was about to jump in when...

"Howwwwwl... Howwwwwl!"

It was the wolf pack returning from their hunt.

"Quick, run Evgeni! Or my pack will eat you!" shouted Galina.

"Goodbye little wolf!" shouted Evgeni, and he galloped away.

Galina raced back inside the den just in time. Her pack brought back some fresh meat from their hunt.

Eat up little Galina, you must be hungry.

Then the pack were off again. Eeew!
"What's that smell?" wondered Galina. She
soon found out, as a big, wet, twitching nose
poked inside the den, drawn by the fresh meat.

"I hope you don't mind if I help myself to some meat," said a smelly wolverine. He was much bigger than Galina, so she thought it was best not to stop him.

"Ah, that's better," said the wolverine. "I haven't eaten for a few days." The wolverine was called Vasili. Galina bravely asked him what thrilling things he had found in the forest.

"You never know what surprises you will find under the snow," said Vasili, whose super sensitive nose could sniff out anything. "And look, I found this tasty meat, and you!"

Suddenly their came a
Howwwwwwwl!
The wolf pack was
coming back.

"Run Vasili! Or my pack will eat you!" shouted Galina. She dragged the meat outside. "If the pack come into the den they will smell that a stranger has been here."

"There's not much meat left," said Galina's mother. "What a big appetite for such a little wolf!"

Some more meat was left for Galina, then the pack went off to hunt again.

Thanks Mum!

Again Galina was left alone. Except she did not feel like she was alone. "Is there anyone there?" she stammered. **"Whooo-ooo-ooo-ooo, whooo-ooo-ooo-ooo!"** came the reply. The forest was scary in the evening.

"Are you going to eat me?" asked Galina, looking at Olga's sharp beak and hooked talons. "Of course not, you're too big for me to eat," said Olga.

"Do you find the forest an exciting place to live?" asked Galina.

"Yes - I always see amazing animals when I'm soaring over the forest," replied Olga.

She fluffed her feathers and went on, "Tigers, reindeer, red foxes, leopards... we are all so different, but we all share the forest."

Galina felt lucky to live among the creatures who shared the forest.

Later, Galina asked her pack
about the wonders of their home.
    "The forest is beautiful, but it
is also important," said her father.
"Did you know it can change
the weather?"

"There is a special thing called carbon in the trees and the frozen soil. If too many trees are chopped down and the carbon escapes, the world may get too hot for everyone."

Wow, Dad! I can't wait to explore our forest when I'm bigger!

The Greedy Jay

Illustrated by
Carolina Coroa

Jutta the jay loved acorns. They were her favourite food.

Every year in autumn, acorns fell from oak trees, and Jutta started collecting and hiding them. She hid hundreds of acorns in secret places all over the forest.

When winter came, and everything was frozen, there were fewer insects, fruit and seeds to eat. Many animals were very hungry.

Jutta was never hungry - she always had more than enough acorns hidden away. But although she had more food than she needed, she would not share it with other animals.

Every day, Jutta flew to each of her hiding places in the forest to check on her acorns. But one morning, something changed.

335

Jutta met an old jay called Jonas. "Can I have one of your acorns?" he asked.

No, go away!

Greedy Jutta did not want to share a single acorn.

When Jutta was sure Jonas
had gone, she scraped away the
snow at the bottom of the tree.

"It's gone!" she cried. One of Jutta's
acorns was missing!

The next day, Jutta flew off
to check her acorns. She landed in
a tree that was one of her
favourite hiding places. A woodpecker,
whose name was Walden, was clinging
to the trunk.

"Please can I have one of your
tasty acorns?" Walden asked.

"No, I need them all!" replied Jutta.

Walden flew off to
search for food elsewhere.
  But when Jutta checked
inside the hidey-hole in the
tree, what did she find?

Noooo!
Another acorn
has gone!

Jutta did not sleep well. She had a bad feeling about her acorn stores. On the third morning she met Rae the red squirrel. Rae also asked Jutta for an acorn.

I don't have enough for myself!

When Rae had scampered away,
Jutta looked under the log she
had been sitting on.

Another
one gone!

She was not surprised that the acorn
she had stashed there was gone. There must
be a thief in the forest!

Jutta set off to find the thief. First she went back to the big beech tree and found Jonas. He was having a nap and dreaming of acorns.

"Have you stolen my acorns?" asked Jutta.

"Mmmm, acorns..." mumbled Jonas.

Then he opened his eyes and saw Jutta's cross face.

"I would never steal," he replied.

Jutta flew
off in search of
Walden the woodpecker.

Tap! Tap!
Tap! Tap!

Tap, tap,
tappity-tap!

Jutta could hear Walden
hammering the trunk with his
beak before she saw him.
Walden did not hear Jutta's
squawks at first.

"Did you steal my acorns?" shouted Jutta.

Hey!
Can you
hear me?

Walden stopped hammering.
"Why are you shouting?" he
asked. "Of course I didn't steal
your acorns."

Jutta set off to look for Rae. She spotted the red squirrel leaping nimbly down a trunk and hovered in her path. But Rae didn't pause, and pushed straight past Jutta.

Hey, mind where you're going!

At Jutta's angry caw, Rae skidded to a halt.

Did YOU steal my acorns?

Who? Me?

Rae glanced a little nervously over Jutta's shoulder. "Of course not," she said.

None of the forest animals Jutta
questioned owned up to stealing her acorns,
so she made a plan to catch the thief.

She chose three of her biggest, tastiest
acorns. Then she carefully scratched little
crosses on them with her beak.

Jutta placed the acorns in a large tree hole.

I'll make it really easy for the thief.

Then she hid at the bottom of the trunk, and waited.

349

Her busy morning had made Jutta feel rather sleepy, and she soon dozed off.

Suddenly she was jolted out of her nap. Something had fallen on her head! It was one of her acorns!

Smack!

350

Stop, thief!

Jutta flew up at once to catch the culprit, and there was Rae! She was picking up the other acorns she had dropped.

These aren't your acorns!

351

"Um… these acorns are mine," said Rae.

But when Jutta showed her the scratches on the acorns, Rae knew she was caught!

I am sorry, but I was so hungry.

Then Jutta felt
sorry for being so mean.
"In winter there is less
food in the forest, so I will
share my acorns with all of
you in future," she said.

The Stubborn Bear

Illustrated by Sian Roberts

"I am not sleepy!" Briana the grizzly cub growled. She did not want to be stuck inside the den with her mother and brother for months over winter.

There's not enough food for us over winter. We must sleep!

But Briana would not listen. She waited
until her mother and brother were fast asleep
then she quietly left the den.

Whoosh!

Outside the snow sparkled!
Briana had forgotten how icy
snow was. As soon as she
stepped outside... whoosh!

She slipped onto her bottom
and tumbled down the mountain,
thump, thumpety-thump!

Luckily for Briana, someone big and soft
was there to stop her fall. It was a reindeer,
whose name was Riley.

"Oops," said Briana
as she fell bottom-
first into Riley.

"What are you doing out on
your own, little bear?" asked Riley.
"I'm going to survive in the forest
over winter," replied Briana.

Briana asked
Riley for tips.
"Lichens are
all the food I need
over winter," said
Riley. "I use my
sharp hooves and
antlers to dig
them up from
under the snow."

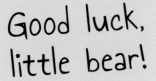

Good luck,
little bear!

"Eew!" Briana
scowled as she
tried Riley's
lichens. "These are
not as sweet as delicious
blueberries. I must find
something sweeter to
eat over winter."

Briana was so busy searching for something to eat that she did not spot Harrison the snowshoe hare, and almost trod on him.

Watch out!

"I didn't see you against the snow," replied Briana.

When both animals had said sorry to each other, Briana asked Harrison for his tips on surviving in the forest over winter.

"My white fur helps me to stay hidden from animals that might eat me," he said. "And my big feet, which look like shoes, help me to hop over the snow."

That's why I'm called a snowshoe hare!

Briana tried hopping just like Harrison, but she was too heavy, and sunk into the soft snow.

"My body is not as good in the snow as yours," she said.

Good luck, little bear!

Harrison hopped on his way. Briana's tummy rumbled and she remembered how hungry she was.

"I'll go to the river and catch some tasty salmon," she said.

But when Briana reached the river she had a surprise. It was frozen!

"I can't catch any salmon here," she cried. "What can I eat in this winter forest?"

Would you like some of my leftover meat?

Briana looked up into a tree, and there was Piper the pine marten. Briana was not sure she would like Piper's food but she was hungry.

The meat was not as tasty as the moths Briana's mother gave her to eat.

"Are there any moths here?" she asked Piper.

"There are no moths in this forest in winter," laughed Piper.

Briana asked Piper
for tips to survive
in the forest.

"This winter forest is no place for a young
cub. Go back to your den," Piper replied. But
Briana felt better after eating something
and she wanted to play.

Piper agreed to play a game of hide-and-seek with Briana.

"But just the one game," said Piper. "As I have trees to climb." She closed her eyes and started counting...

"one...

two...

three...

"... fifty... coming!"

Where could Briana hide? She thought about following the river but she might get lost or slip in through the ice. Best to go back through the part of the forest she knew.

Piper was on Briana's trail. Briana needed to find a hiding place. It was not easy running over the snow and she wished she had Harrison's big furry feet.

"There is nowhere to hide behind these bare trees," said Briana. "And my paw prints in the snow are giving me away."

She **slipped, skidded** and **sank** in the snow and ran head first into... Harrison!

"Quick, this way," whispered Harrison. "Hide in here. I can run fast and will lead Piper away from you. She will think my paw prints belong to you."

But you don't look like me!

Harrison pulled some lichen over his white fur so it looked more like Briana's fur from a distance.

"Over here!" he shouted in a big, growly voice like Briana's, and then he was off.

From a distance, Harrison looked like Briana, and Piper was fooled. But when Piper stopped to catch her breath she looked closer at the paw print trail.

Those are not Briana's paw prints. I've been tricked!

Briana left her hiding place and ran through the forest again. But Piper was not far behind.

You can't catch me!

Yes I can!

The shouting woke up
Riley who was napping nearby.

"Come here!" she shouted as she quickly
scooped out a snow hole for Briana to hide in.

But Piper was
not fooled this time.

RAAAA!

Just as Piper was about to catch Briana, an enormous roar echoed in the forest, and a gigantic grizzly bear appeared. It was Briana's mother, looking for her.

Briana was happy to be back in her warm den. She was sorry for being stubborn and not listening to her mother.

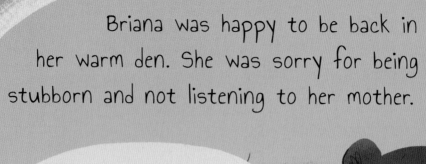

Now do you see why we bears need to sleep over winter? Sleep well, little bear.

Briana's new friends had run away as they did not want to be eaten by a big grizzly bear, but Briana would see them again in the springtime after her long winter sleep.

ZZZZ